SUPERBOT

> There is naughtiness all around us!

Superbot and the Terrible Toy Destroyer
is a DAVID FICKLING BOOK

First published in Great Britain in 2016
by David Fickling Books,
31 Beaumont Street,
Oxford, OX1 2NP

Text and illustrations © Nick Ward, 2016

978-1-910200-30-8

1 3 5 7 9 10 8 6 4 2

David Fickling Books supports the Forest Stewardship Council® (FSC®),
the leading international forest certification organisation.
All our titles that are printed on Greenpeace-approved
FSC-certified paper carry the FSC logo.

MIX
Paper from
responsible sources
FSC® C104723

DAVID FICKLING BOOKS Reg. No. 8340307
A CIP catalogue record for this book is available from the British Library.

Printed in China by Toppan Leefung.

SUPERBOT

AND THE
TERRIBLE TOY DESTROYER!

NICK WARD

David Fickling Books

CHAPTER 1
SOS!

Superbot
Specifications

- **Materials:** Tin, wire, glue and plastic
- **Height:** 114 cm/45 inches
- **Weight:** 22.6 kg/50 lb
- **Top Speed:** Running – 80 mph; flying – 220 mph
- **Super-fast computer brain:** 3.4 GHz Brainy Core Processor, 8 GB memory, 1500 MHz DDR3
- **Strength:** Can crush a can with his bare hands and lift a boulder above his head

Signature: MWs Brightspark
(Inventor)

Bot the Super Robot lives with his inventor, Mrs Brightspark, in their secret headquarters on top of a very tall skyscraper.

Bot can run as fast as a speeding train and fly faster than a roaring jet.

He can see for miles and miles and do very hard sums with his computer brain.

$24 \times$
$32 +$
7×22
$+ 174$
$\div 3$
$+ 27$
$\times 64$
$+ 297$
$- 82 +$
$436 \div 9$
$+ 22 \times 4$
$= 164454$
37037

Mrs Brightspark!

BLUEPRINT FOR SUPERBOT

Botdriver

Botcatapult

Stun gun

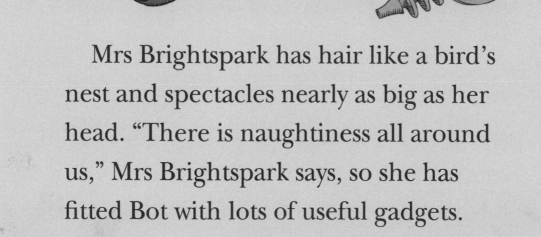

Mrs Brightspark has hair like a bird's nest and spectacles nearly as big as her head. "There is naughtiness all around us," Mrs Brightspark says, so she has fitted Bot with lots of useful gadgets.

Telescopic sight

Botblaster

One day, Bot's Trouble Tracking System started to hum and the radar screen flashed.

"Calling Bot. SOS!" said a crackly voice from the loudspeaker. "Bruto the Bad is on the rampage." Bruto was a robot too, a GIANT robot, and one of Bot's worst enemies. He was always up to no good.

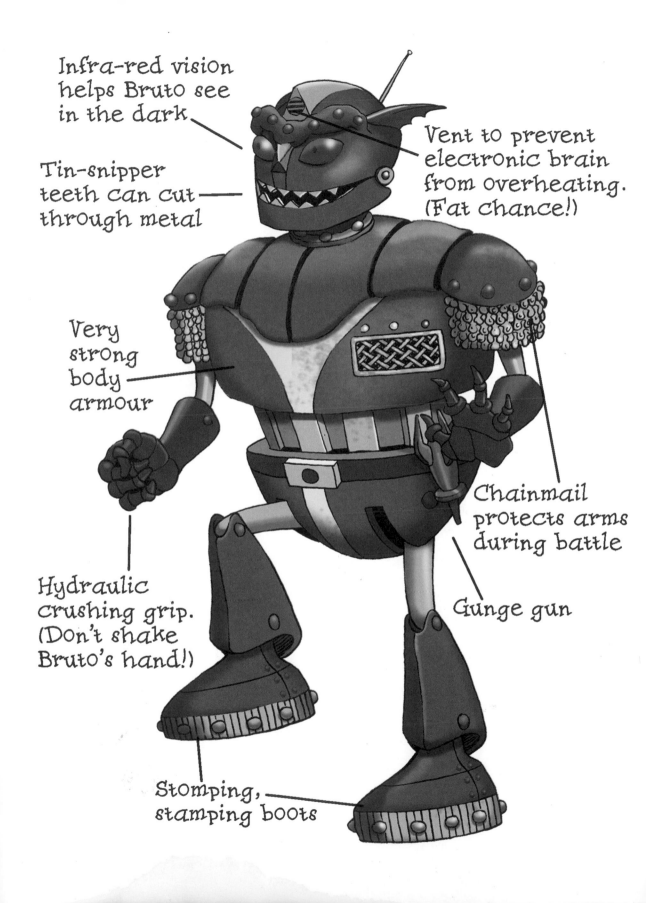

Infra-red vision helps Bruto see in the dark

Tin-snipper teeth can cut through metal

Vent to prevent electronic brain from overheating. (Fat chance!)

Very strong body armour

Chainmail protects arms during battle

Hydraulic crushing grip. (Don't shake Bruto's hand!)

Gunge gun

Stomping, stamping boots

"Do be careful, Bot," said Mrs Brightspark, hurrying from the kitchen and handing him his oil can.

"Make sure you're home in time for refuelling."

She was covered in flour from baking Bot's favourite nut cakes. Yummy!

Bot took a glug from his oil can for
extra energy and ran across the roof of
the skyscraper.

He pressed a button and a rocket
pack unfolded from his back. With a
burst of flame the rockets roared into
life.

Bot leaped from the edge of the
building and zoomed across the sky.

"Up and away," he cried. "*Fizz, ping!*
Bot to the rescue!"

CHAPTER 2

Bruto the Bad!

Bot soared over rooftops, scanning the streets with his telescopic vision. In the distance he spotted Bruto the Bad marching into the park.

Bruto was carrying a big
sack over his
shoulder.
A crowd of
children was
chasing
after
him.

"That's Lucy and her
friends," said Bot, and he
turned up his super-sensitive
hearing to listen.

14

"Give us back our toys!" he heard Lucy say.

"Nah!" said Bruto in a booming voice. He tipped the sack upside down and a pile of toys fell out. He stuffed a handful into his mouth and crunched them into tiny pieces.

As the giant robot grabbed another fistful of toys, Lucy jumped up and clung to the leg of a scrappy teddy bear.

GNARR!

Fizz, ping!

"You're not eating my teddy," she shouted bravely.

Let go!

"*Fizz, ping!* Bot to the rescue!" cried Bot, and swooped out of the sky.

He took the super-duper Botblaster
from his tummy hatch. As Bruto raised
the toys and Lucy in the air, dropping
them into his open mouth, Bot fired.

Just in time!

WHOOSH!

A net shot from the blaster. It sailed
through the air, wrapped itself around
Lucy and her teddy, and whisked
them out of Bruto's crushing jaws.

"You!" growled Bruto menacingly, shaking his iron fist at Bot.

"It's Superbot!" cried Lucy, as a parachute opened on the net and she began to drift towards the ground.

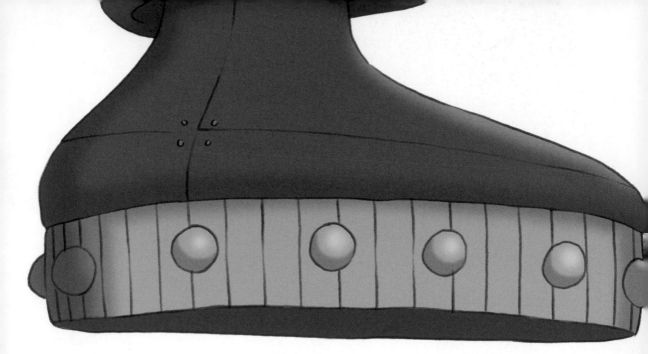

"Help us, Bot! Bruto's taken all
our toys," said Ben.

"He opened my bedroom window,
reached inside and stole my wooden
castle," cried Daisy.

"*Zzz, ping!* Give back their toys," said
Bot, but Bruto stamped his giant feet
and began squashing the toys
as flat as pancakes.

Then he snatched Lucy out of the air and ran off with her.

"Put me down, you overgrown tin can," called Lucy. "Help me, Bot!"

Bot zoomed after them.

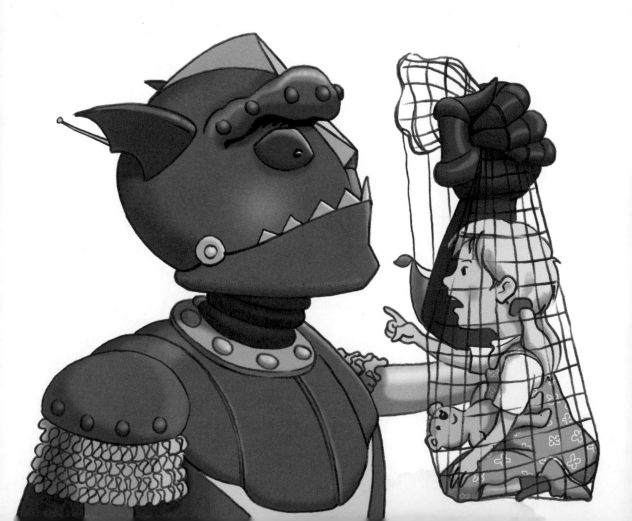

"STOP!"** shouted Bot, racing in front of the giant robot. Bruto roared like an engine and his eyes glowed red. A laser beam shot from each eye.

Bot whizzed out of the way and fired
his stun gun, but Bruto lifted a massive
hand and swatted Bot like a fly.

"*Whir-whizz-fizz!*" cried Bot.

He went spinning through the air like
a Catherine wheel and crashed to the
ground.

His rockets were bent out of shape,
and when he tried to restart them they
spluttered and coughed.

Bot flicked a switch on his chest and
with a low hum his boots became magnetic.
He ran straight up Bruto's metal back
and sat astride his broad shoulders. Bot
unscrewed a panel at the back of Bruto's
head with his whizzo Botdriver. It sprang
open and Bot reached inside for Bruto's
power switch.

"*Bzzz, fizz!* Put Lucy down," said Bot.
"Or I will turn off your main circuit."
"Oh, nuts and bolts!" moaned Bruto,
and put Lucy back on the ground.

Grrrumble!

The metal monster sat down with a heavy clunk and started to make the strangest noises.

"What is he doing?" whispered Lucy, as the big robot's insides gurgled and squealed and two black drops of oil splashed to the ground.

Fizz, clang!

"I think he's crying," said Bot.

"Stop it Bruto," said Lucy. "What's the matter?"

"Want Freddie," wailed the monster robot, his jaws squeaking and squealing.

"*What* is Freddie?" asked Lucy.

"Freddie the Fiery Dragon. My favourite toy," said Bruto in a metallic drone. "Can't find him."

"Well, we haven't got him," said Lucy. "And now you've crunched all our toys."

"Waah!" wailed Bruto, rubbing his oily eyes.

Boo-hoo!

"Never fear, Bot is here," said the little Super Robot. "If you promise to be good, *fizz, clang,* I'll find Freddie for you."

"P-p-promise?" stuttered the iron giant, sniffing.

Bot flipped back the top of his head and a little spinning propeller popped out. It lifted him high into the air.

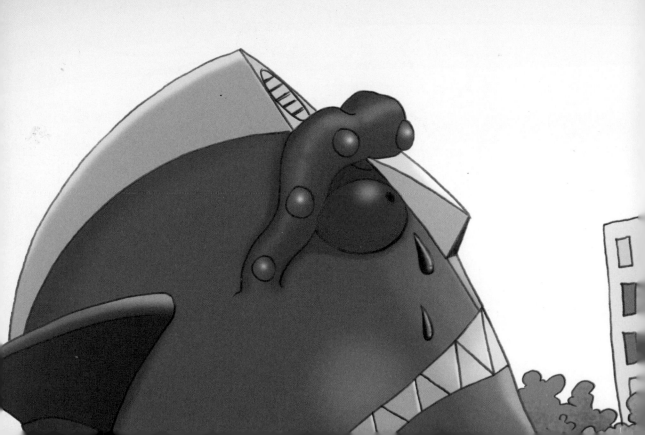

Then his radar transmitter began to
send out radio waves in search of
Bruto's lost toy.

Beep . . .
Beep . . .
Beep!

Mini helicopter blades

Flip top

Radar
transmitter

Radar
aerial

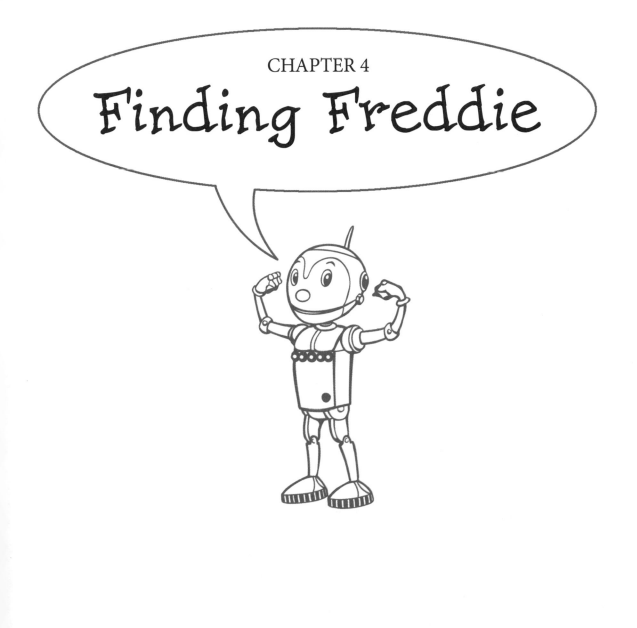

CHAPTER 4

Finding Freddie

Bot studied the screen on his Botpad.
Pictures started to form of all the
things his radar could find – a scruffy dog,
a lost glove and a snuffling hedgehog.

Then the image of a little fiery
dragon appeared on the screen.
It was in a twiggy nest at the top of a
tall tree, and a huge black and white
bird was standing guard over it. It was
Magwitch the Magpie.

"*Fzzz!* So that's where it's got to,"
said Bot.

He knew magpies loved to collect
sparkly things, and the toy dragon must
have been too shiny to resist. "Follow
me," he said, and buzzed across the park
like a mini helicopter.

magwitch
loves shiny
things!

Whirrr!

Bot flew right to the top of the tree.

"Excuse me. Could you give Bruto his dragon back, please?" he asked.

"*Naw!*" cawed Magwitch, giving Bot a withering look.

40

"Bruto might get angry and shake your nest out of the tree," warned Bot, but with a squawk the magpie launched himself at the surprised robot and chased him away.

"*Emergency!*" cried Bot, as Magwitch snapped at his heels with his sharp, clacking beak.

Then he remembered the pocket
money that Mrs Brightspark gave him
each week to buy himself treats.

He opened his tummy hatch
and took out a shiny coin.

"Look, Magwitch!" he said, and with
his powerful Bot catapult he fired it far
into the distance. The coin flashed in
the sunlight as it spun through the air.

"*Caw!*" cried Magwitch, hypnotised by its brilliance, and greedily raced after it.

Bot hurried back to the nest, grabbed the tin dragon and flew down to where Bruto and Lucy were waiting.

"Freddie!" cried Bruto, as Bot
handed him his toy. He turned the key
in the dragon's back and clapped his
hands as it rolled across the grass.

"What about *our* toys, Bruto?" asked
Lucy, as Tom and the rest of her friends
rushed over to see if she was all right.

Bruto's insides buzzed and popped and crackled. "Sorry," he droned.

"I know," said Bot. He ran over to the pile of squashed toys and put them into Bruto's sack.

Fizz, Ping!

"Mrs Brightspark
will fix these,"
he said.
"Hooray!" cheered
Lucy and her friends.
All of a sudden Bot
started to feel weary.
A red light on his
chest blinked.
"Oh dear, I need
refuelling," he said,
his buzzing robot
voice beginning
to slow down.
"I'd better . . .
hurry . . . home."

"I'll help," said Bruto in his deep, echoey voice, and he picked up the heavy sack.

"Thank . . . *bzzz* . . . you," said Bot.

"Bye, Bot. Bye, Bruto," the children called.

"*Caw!*" complained Magwitch, who had just returned with the shiny coin.

Bot hurried home, before his energy ran out.

49

CHAPTER 5

Home Sweet Home

"**W**ell done," said Mrs Brightspark when Bot had finished telling his story. He'd been refuelled with nut cakes, Mrs Brightspark had repaired his

rocket boosters and they were sitting at
the kitchen table being very busy. Mrs
Brightspark was mending the children's
toys, and Bot was oiling his joints.

"I wonder if Bruto will be a good robot from now on," Bot said.

"Who knows? There is naughtiness all around us, Bot," said Mrs Brightspark. "That's why I invented you. A Super Robot that tracks down baddies everywhere."

Just then, Bot's Trouble Tracking System started to beep.

"Calling Bot. SOS!"

There is naughtiness all around us, Bot.

"*Fzzz!* Oh, dear," said Bot, running into his room and checking the screen. "Terrible Toad is being very naughty!"

"Not Terrible Toad," gasped Mrs Brightspark. "You'd better hurry. But make sure you're home before bedtime."

BOOM!

Bot ran out of their headquarters,
leaped from the edge of the skyscraper
and zoomed across the sky.

"Bot to the rescue!" he cried.

BOIP!

Who is Terrible Toad?
What is he up to with his
Goo Extractor, and will Bot
put a stop to his naughtiness?

Look out for the next
exciting installment of

SUPERBOT